The Royal Baby-Sitters

by Joy Cowley

The king and the queen
didn't have any children.
They knew nothing about babies.
They said they would look after
their cook's baby girl
for one night
while the cook went out.

2

"She's a very quiet baby," said the cook.
"She'll be no trouble at all.
I'll be back tomorrow at lunchtime."

The king and the queen
played with the baby
for a couple of hours.
Then, for no reason at all,
the baby began to cry.

"Quick! Do something!" said the queen.

"Like what?" said the king.

"Like some more dinner!"
the queen replied.

But the baby didn't want more dinner.
She cried and cried.

"Let's give her something to look at," said the queen.

"Good thinking!" said the king. "How about TV?"

They took the crying baby into the royal TV room. There were ten TVs going, each on a different channel. They took the cook's baby from one TV to another to make her stop crying.

The baby was crying so hard
she didn't even look at them.

"What's the opposite of crying?"
said the king.

"Laughing?" asked the queen.

"Right the first time," said the king.
"I'm going to phone the circus.
I'll ask them to come
and perform for us.
That'll make the baby laugh."

But the circus didn't work either.

The baby went on crying
while the jugglers juggled
and the clowns clowned.
She went on crying
while the tigers chewed the curtains.
She went on crying
while the elephant sat on the throne
and broke it.

In the end, the king and queen
felt like crying, too.

"Send that circus away!"
they ordered.

The king and queen
didn't know what to do next.

"What about music?" someone said.
So the army band was called.

The men and women
stood around the baby
and played their trumpets and drums.
Still the baby cried.
The band played louder
and LOUDER
and **L O U D E R .**

The baby roared back.

The king and queen were exhausted.
"Send for the doctor," said the queen.

The doctor took one look
at the king and the queen
and the band and the baby.

"There's only one thing wrong
with this baby," the doctor said.
"She's tired. It's past her bedtime.
Stop all this noise
and let her go to sleep!"

The army band stopped playing.
"Tired," said the king, and he yawned.
"Sleep," said the queen, and she nodded.
The men and the women
put down their trumpets and drums.
"It's past our bedtime, too,"
they said.

When the cook came home
the next day at lunchtime,
there they all were,
still fast asleep.